RiTA THE RESCUER

AND ~~OTHER STORI~~ES

RiTA THE RESCUER

AND OTHER STORIES

HILDA OFFEN

Catnip

For Daisy and Tom

CATNIP BOOKS
Published by Catnip Publishing Ltd
Quality Court, off Chancery Lane
London WC2A 1HR

Rita the Rescuer first published 1996 by Puffin and 2002 by Happy Cat Books
Rita and the Haunted House first published 2004 by Happy Cat Books
Rita and the Deep Blue Sea first published 2005 by Happy Cat Books

This edition first published 2012
3 5 7 9 10 8 6 4 2

A CIP catalogue record for this book is available from the British Library

ISBN 978-1-84647-151-3

Printed in Poland

www.catnippublishing.co.uk

Contents

Rita the Rescuer

There are four children in the Potter family – Eddie, Julie, Jim and Rita.

Because Rita is the youngest, the others sometimes leave her out of their games. They say they have to spend all their time rescuing Rita – she falls in the mud, she gets stuck up trees and she loses her Wellingtons. Poor Rita!

'Take me with you!' begged Rita one day.

'You're too young!' said Eddie. 'You can't push or pull.'

'You're too young!' said Julie. 'You can't skip or jump.'

'You're too young!' said Jim. 'You can't run or kick.'

Eddie, Julie and Jim went off to play
with their friends. Rita was left alone with
the cat.

'You'd like some milk, wouldn't you?'
said Rita and she went to get it in from
the doorstep.

'What's this?' she cried. 'A parcel – for
me?'

Rescuer's Outfit said the label inside

First Rita unpacked some boots, then gloves and tights, a tunic, a belt and a cloak.

'Oh!' she said. 'That's just what I need.'

And she put them all on as fast as she could.

In the street some children were jumping over a rope.

'Let me try!' said Rita.

'You're too young!' they said and they held the rope even higher.

But Rita wasn't put off.
She drew a deep breath, gave
a hop, step and jump and –
up she soared!

Rita could hardly believe
what was happening.
'Look at me! Look at me!'
she shouted.

Rita's leap carried her high above the rooftops. She could see for miles. Down in the next street she spotted Basher Briggs who was snatching her brother Jim's football.

GIVE THAT FOOTBALL BACK!

Rita's roar was so loud that all the windows round about rattled.

Basher turned pale.

'I'm off!' he said and he dropped the football and ran away as fast as he could.

'Thanks a lot,' said Jim.

'You're welcome!' said Rita. 'Now for my next rescue!'

She could hear someone close by yelling, 'Help! Help!'

A pram had rolled into the river. Worse still, there was a baby inside! The current was sweeping it away and no one would reach it.

Quick as a flash, Rita
dived into the water.
She grasped the pram
firmly and swam to the
river bank.

The ducks quacked
and the people cheered.

The mother hugged
her baby and shook
Rita's hand.

'You deserve a
medal!' she said.

Rita was about to reply when she heard a scream. There, on the other side of the river, was her sister Julie.

She was being chased by a bull!

In a split second, Rita was there.

She flung herself in front of the bull, who stopped dead in his tracks.

'Bull – you're a bully!' said Rita.

She stared straight into his little red eyes, while Julie escaped over a gate.

The bull looked ashamed and shuffled his hooves; but Rita was already on her way.

It was Lavinia Smith's wedding day.
There she was, with her flower and her
bridesmaids – but the car had a flat tyre.
Mrs Smith looked furious and Mr Smith
was in a panic.

'Oh no, the foot pump doesn't work!'
he cried.

Rita came bounding over a hedge.

'Leave this to me, Mr Smith,' she said. 'It won't take a minute.'

She gave a mighty puff.

'There you are. That's fixed it!' she said.

'Thank goodness for the Rescuer!' cried Lavinia as the car roared away down the street.

Nearby in Jubilee
Gardens a huge
crowd had gathered
beneath a tree.

'That cat's going to
fall!' someone yelled.

'Our poor little
Rufus!' cried Mr and
Mrs Rumbold.

'Hang on, Rufus!'
called Rita. 'Here I
come!'

She whooshed
through the air like
a whirlwind.

'Ooh!' gasped the
crowd.

'Got you!' said Rita
and she snatched
Rufus to safety just as
his claws slipped from
the branch.

'Thank you! Thank you!' cried Mr and Mrs Rumbold, but Rita was off again – she had heard another call for help. Eddie's go-cart was out of control and hurtling down the steepest hill in town.

Rita ran like a greyhound.

She grabbed the go-cart and braked so hard with her heels that sparks flew in the air.

'Phew!' said Eddie, as they screeched to a halt. 'That was a very close thing!'

At the foot of the hill a crowd stood and stared.

Mr Carter's mare, Rosie, had fallen down a hole in the road. No one knew how to get her out.

But help was at hand.

Speeding down the street came
– a jet plane?
– a javelin?
– a flash of greased lightning?
No! It was Rita the Rescuer.

Rita dived down into the hole.
'One – two – three – heave!' she cried.
She raised Rosie above her head.
'Up you go!' she said and she lifted Rosie
out of the hole and placed her back
safely on the road.

'What strength!' cried the crowd.
'What muscles! Did you ever see anything
like it?'

They cheered and they clapped and
Rosie swished her tail.

'Goodbye, everybody!' said Rita.
'I'm off home for my tea!'

But she stopped on her way to hit two
thousand runs –

to kick four hundred goals –

and to skip to three thousand and eighty.

'What a busy day,' said Rita, back home in her room. She took off the Rescuer outfit and hid it under her bed.

'Everyone's talking about the Rescuer!'
said Eddie at teatime. 'She terrific! Who can
she be?'

'Where can she come from?' asked Julie.

'However does she do those rescues?' cried
Jim.

Rita could have told them, but her secret
was special. So she smiled to herself, picked
up her spoon, and started eating her beans.

Rita and the Haunted House

'We're going Trick or Treating with
Tania's dad,' said Julie.

'And after that,' said Eddie, 'we're going
to the Parkers'. They're having a Haunted
House party.'

'Can I come?' asked Rita.

'You'd be scared!' said Julie. 'There'll be
ghosts!'

'And witches! And monsters!' said Jim.

'Please!' begged Rita.
'No,' said Eddie. 'You'll be safer here.'
'Please! Please! Please!' cried Rita.

'No way!' said Julie; and they shoved the pumpkin on Rita's head and ran off. Rita stumbled round and round in circles and tripped over the cat.

I'll show them! thought Rita; and she ran upstairs and put on her Rescuer outfit.

She looked out of the window.

Huh! There's Basher Briggs! she thought. *Up to no good as usual.*

Basher was diguised as a vampire and he was frightening old ladies on their way to Bingo.

Yaargh!

Help!

Rita swooped down and whistled.

Hundreds of rats ran out of the shadows and surrounded Basher.

'Keep him here!' said Rita. 'Make sure he doesn't move.'

Then she was off.

In the next street the Trick or Treaters were knocking at a door.

'Trick or Treat!' called Julie.

'Trick!' yelled Basher Briggs' grandma and she hurled a bucket of icy water over them.

Time to use my secret Sweet Rays! thought Rita. *Here we go!*

The water froze in mid-air. Then it turned into a shower of sweets and fell to earth.

'Hooray!' cried the Trick or Treaters. 'Thank you, Rescuer!'

Rita flew on. She'd heard a strange sound.

Some big green monsters were knocking
at a window. Every time the Turner family
looked out the monsters pulled horrible
faces and roared 'Boo!' The Turners were
in a panic.

Rita crept round to the back door.
'Let me in!' she called through the cat-
flap. 'I'm here to help.'
'Are we glad to see you, Rescuer!' gasped
Mr Turner.

Rita marched up to the window.
'Open the curtains!' she said. 'Now!'
'BOOOO!' she roared as the curtains
swished back.

'Aargh!' squealed the monsters. 'It's the Rescuer! Let's get out of here!'

And they charged away into the distance.

'Oh, thank you, Rescuer!' cried Mr Turner. 'Have a toffee apple!'

'Thanks,' said Rita. 'But I think I'm needed in the park.'

'Hoooo! Woof woof! Hoooo-ooo!'

A little werewolf had caught his tail in the slide. Rita untangled him and he slid down.

'Boo-hoo!' he whimpered.

'What's the matter?' asked Rita.

'I wish I wasn't a werewolf!' he snuffled. 'I'm a boy in the daytime but at night I have to run around scaring people. I don't like it. I get really lonely.'

'Watch this!' said Rita. 'Don't take your eyes off it.'

She swung her belt buckle backwards and forwards and she spoke very slowly.

'You – will – give – up – werewolfing,' she said. 'From – now – on – you – will – be – an – ordinary – boy.'

She snapped her fingers and the werewolf
turned back into little Joey Harper.
'Come on,' said Rita. 'I'll see you home.'

Rita dropped Joey at his house.
'Hello!' she said. 'What's all that
screaming coming from next door?'

A ghost was on the loose in the Haunted House – and what was worse, it was a real ghost!

Everyone was terrified. The ghost floated round the room, flapping its arms and wailing, 'Whooo!'

Rita jumped through the window.

'Can't catch me!' said the ghost.
'Whoooo-ooo!'
'We'll see about that!' said Rita.
The ghost floated through a wall; and
so did Rita. Then it floated through the
ceiling; and Rita followed it.

'Whoooo-hoooo!' wailed the ghost and it shot up the chimney; but Rita was close behind.

Rita chased the ghost round and round
the chimney stack until at last the ghost
collapsed in a heap and gasped, 'I give up!
You win!'

'Then off you go!' said Rita 'And keep
going.'

The ghost gave a shriek and flew away;
and it didn't stop until it reached
the moon.

'Kitty, Kitty, Kitty!'
Julie was stroking a cat.
'I wonder who you
belong to?' she said.
She soon found out.
A witch swooped down
on her broomstick.

She snatched the cat in one hand and Julie in the other and streaked off through the night sky.

'We'll be late for the witches' party!' she cackled.

'I'm not a real witch!' screamed Julie. 'Let me go!'

But the witch took no notice.

Rita zoomed after them. She grabbed the broomstick and shook it.

The witch fell into a holly bush and her cat fell on top of her.

Rita caught Julie and flew her back to the Haunted House; and she performed some amazing feats on the way.

Rita parked the broomstick by the front door.

'Boo-hoo-hoo!' The sound was coming from the front room.

'What's going on here?' asked Rita.

Can I have your auto-graph?

Sorry — I'm needed indoors.

'I was telling them a story,' said Mr
Parker. 'And they started to cry. We'd just
got to the bit where the big red-eyed
monster jumps out of a cupboard.'

'BOO-HOO!' roared the children, more
loudly than ever. Rita raised her hand
and they stopped. 'Don't be scared!' she
said. 'Everything was all right in the end –
because I came along!'

The children smiled and started to clap.
'Oh, thanks, Rescuer,' said Mr Parker.
'Would you like to stay for some apple-
bobbing?'

So Rita did; and she just had time to
judge the fancy-dress competition before
she went home.

First Prize goes to the pumpkin!

By the time the others came back Rita was in her pyjamas.

'Look, Rita – we've bought you a toffee apple!' said Eddie. 'And some vampire teeth.'

'You missed the Rescuer again!' said Jim. 'She was fantastic! She stopped us from getting soaked.'

'She chased away a ghost!' said Julie. 'And she saved me from a witch.'

Rita licked her toffee apple.

'Did she?' she said. 'She must be really, really brave.'

Rita in the
Deep Blue Sea

'It's nice to be somewhere hot for a change,' said Mrs Potter.

'Where's Grandad? And Eddie and Julie and Jim?' asked Rita.

'Oh, they've gone for a boat ride,' said Mrs Potter.

'I wanted to go!' said Rita.

'You're too young,' said Mrs Potter. 'You stay here and do some paddling.'

Rita watched the boat disappear over the horizon. Suddenly all the children in the sea started to cry. A big octopus had sneaked up and stolen their ice creams.

It's a good job I brought my Rescuer outfit, thought Rita.

She grabbed her beach bag and ran
behind the windbreak. In the blink of an
eye she'd turned into Rita the Rescuer.

'Here I come!' she called and dived into
the water.

Rita chased the octopus out to sea. Then she played a clever trick on him. Soon the octopus was tied in knots. Rita rolled him miles away from the shore.

'Please undo me!' begged the octopus.

'Only if you promise to behave yourself in future,' said Rita.

'I promise! I promise!' cried the octopus.

So Rita untangled him. Just as she untied the last knot something caught her eye.

A scuba diver had been trapped by a giant clam. He struggled and struggled but it was no use – he was caught fast.

Rita moved like a flash of light. She prised the clam apart and the scuba diver shot to the surface.

'Climb aboard, Rescuer,' said a passing turtle. 'I'll take you to the coral reef.'

A glass-sided submarine glided by. The tourists inside stared and pointed. Just at that moment there was a juddering noise. The engine had broken down! Everyone started to panic.

Rita dived under the submarine and lifted it above her head. Then she carried it to the surface.

The captain looked out.

'Can you mend the engine, Rescuer?' he asked. So Rita grabbed a spanner and in no time at all the submarine was on its way.

'I think you're needed on the sea bed again, Rescuer,' said the turtle.

The scuba diver's friends were exploring the wreck of the *Mary Jane*. Oh no! They had been trapped by a giant eel.

Rita tickled the eel and it wriggled and giggled so much it let the divers go. It slithered away through the porthole.

Ah ha! Another job for the Rescuer, thought Rita, looking over her shoulder.

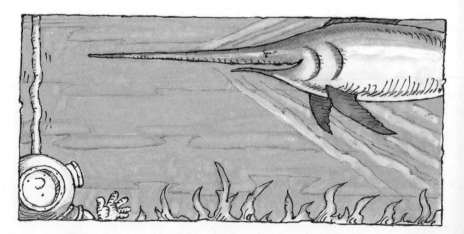

A swordfish was swimming towards a
deep-sea diver. Worse still, it was aiming
straight for his air-line! Rita didn't waste
a minute. She grabbed a piece of wood
from the wreck and swam at the swordfish.
Thud! She was just in the nick of time.
The swordfish's sword stuck in the wood.
Rita and the diver shook hands and the
swordfish swam away.

Above them something blotted out the
sunlight. It was a gigantic fish! It opened
its mouth – and there, right above it, were
Grandad, Eddie, Julie and Jim in their little
boat.

'Must go!' said Rita.

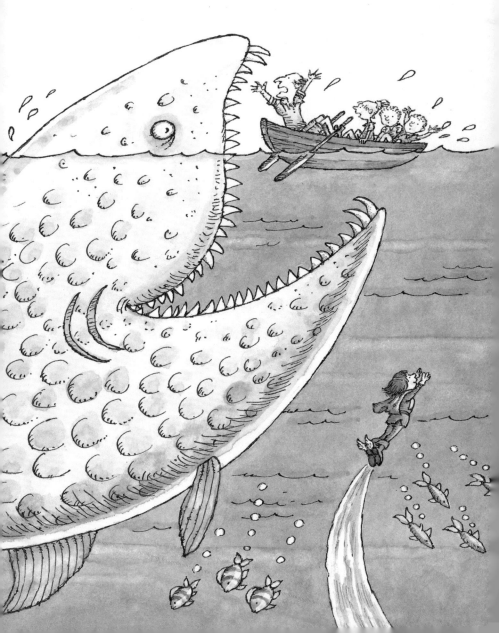

'Gulp!' the fish swallowed the boat whole.
There was no time to lose. Rita dived
straight in after them. She grabbed the boat
and pushed it out again. Then they whizzed
through the sea like a torpedo until they
were well out of harm's way. The fish
flicked its tail and dived to the bottom of
the ocean.

Rita felt something tickling her leg. It was a little mermaid.

'Hello!' she said. 'What can I do for you?'

'Please help us, Rescuer,' said the mermaid. 'A sea monster has captured our treasure. He's sitting on it and he won't go away.'

'We'll see about that!' said Rita.
She followed the mermaid to the mouth of a cave. Inside, they could see the sea monster glaring at them. He'd caught two mermaids and he was licking his lips.

'Yum! Yum!' said the monster.
'Let those mermaids go!' roared Rita.
She pointed her fingers at the monster and zapped him with her sonic shockwaves.

'Ow!' said the monster and the
mermaids darted off.

Then Rita pulled a horrible face. The monster was terrified. He gave a great bubbly roar and swam away as fast as he could.

'Oh, thank you, Rescuer!' cried the
mermaids. They were so grateful they gave
Rita a sparkly tiara from their treasure
chest.

'How kind!' said Rita. 'But I must go. I'm
needed somewhere else.'

A giant sting-ray was about to attack some swimmers.

Whoosh! Rita grabbed the ray and carried it far out to sea.

After that she freed four little seahorses
who were trapped in a jam-jar. And last
of all she untangled a dolphin who'd got
caught in some fishing nets.

'Thanks, Rescuer,' said the dolphin.
'Would you like a lift?'

So Rita rode home on the dolphin's back
and everyone cheered and clapped as they
leaped over the waves.

'That was a good day's work,' said Rita,
and she zoomed up the beach. She darted
behind the windbreak and changed back
into little Rita Potter.

'We were swallowed by a whale!' called
Julie, as the others leaped out of their boat.

'Oh dear!' said Mrs Potter.

'But it was all right,' said Eddie, 'because
the Rescuer turned up and saved us.'

'She always seems to be there when we
need her,' said Jim.

'Where did you get that tiara, Rita?'
asked Julie.

'Oh, a mermaid gave it to me,' said Rita;
and everybody laughed.

Other Rita the Rescuer stories available
with full-colour pictures:

Rita and the Romans
Rita at Rushybrook Farm
Rita in Rocky Park

For more information about these
and other Catnip titles visit:
www.catnippublishing.co.uk